To *Friends* and the Power of Friendship!

A CatFish Tale

By Kathy Brod

A Horse Named Special

By Kathy Br

STOVER

By Kath

The Winner Is...

Kathy Br

Purrsnikitty

By Kathy Brod

just sniffing around

By Kathy Bro

the **Inside** Story

By Kathy

My Bent Tree

by Kathy Brod

A CatFish Tale

Loosely Based on a True Story

By Kathy Brodsky

Illustrations by Cameron Bennett

I'm a regular *cat*
with a tale to tell

about three fish
I know quite well.

My friend **Charlie**
　　　had some fish in a tank.

The fish were his friends—
Gretchen, *Suzie*, and **Hank**.

Charlie's fish were
a good part of his life.

He hardly went out—
had no children or wife.

One day **Charlie** had
a great **INSPIRATION...**

He'd get a college degree!
There was no hesitation.

He researched some schools,
and came up with a few.

A school in Wisconsin,
yes, Wisconsin would do.

Wisconsin was *far*
from our Cape Cod town,

but **Charlie** was eager
to get started, settle down.

But what of his pals
Gretchen, Suzie, and Hank?
He would leave them behind
in their heated fish tank.

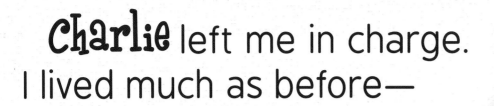

Charlie left me in charge.
I lived much as before—

but temptation was lurking
behind that closed door.

While feeding and taking
good care of the fish

I pictured them all
    lined up in a dish!

YIKES!

One day I came home
and found a *surprise!*

Tiny fish were swimming
with the older big guys.

What should I do?
I bought a fish pen

that would keep them inside
to protect them **and then...**

Many more babies
        arrived as years passed.

New tanks were needed.
    They outgrew them quite fast.

At last I decided
enough was enough

of **cleaning** and *feeding*
and all of that stuff.

BESIDES... I am a cat,
as it's plain to see.

Cats love to eat fish
and I'm getting H-U-N-G-R-Y!

I called my friend Charlie
in that town far away.

I told him I'd be there
within a few days.

How would I take them?
I couldn't drive.

My legs are too **short**—
but... the fish had to arrive!

I bundled each fish
    with its own family

in containers and bags
    to accompany me.

I hired a driver,
      drove part way one day,

spent the night at an inn,
      sneaked in the back way...

Was afraid to get caught—
    pets weren't allowed.

But I had to deliver
    the fish and *right now!*

The next day we got there.
The fish did survive—

and **Charlie** was glad
that his friends were *alive!*

Now that the fish
       are back with their dad

I'm alone in my house,
       kind of **happy... yet sad.**

They were my friends, too.
Fish are good company.
Maybe it's time for...

a PUPPY...

or TWO...

just for me!

FRIENDS

1. What is a friend?

2. How are your friends like you and how are your friends different from you?

3. How can people who are different from one another still be friends?

4. How do you show someone you are a good friend?

5. What do friends do for one another?

6. List qualities and reasons that make your friends special to you.

RESPONSIBILITY

1. What does responsibility mean?

2. How do you show that you are responsible?
   a. at home   b. at school   c. with friends

TEMPTATION

1. Tell about a time when you were tempted to do something you knew you shouldn't.

2. What was it and what happened?

GEOGRAPHY

1 If you live in the United States, look at a map, find your state and notice what states border your state.

2 Can you find the peninsula known as Cape Cod? (Hint – look at the State of Massachusetts.) How far it is from Wisconsin?

3 If you were to drive from Cape Cod to Wisconsin, what are some states you might travel through?

4 If you live outside of the United States, notice what provinces or countries are near you. Plan how you would get to Cape Cod or Wisconsin from where you live.

FUNTIVITY

Thinking about friendship, responsibility, resisting temptation, or geography...

a. write a story or play   b. make up a poem

c. draw a picture   d. make a card and give it to a friend

OR

e. sing a song about any of these — or several of them together.

Who would have thought
that going on vacation would lead to another book?

I hadn't planned to write one after **A Horse Named Special**, but an amazing, true story "fell into my lap." It was too good to pass up.

I was on Cape Cod, and a man told me the following story:

He had befriended a Russian physician who wanted to work as a doctor in the United States, but to become licensed in this country she had to take university courses. The school she chose was in Wisconsin—far from Cape Cod. She left her pet fish with the friend who promised to care for them. But the fish soon multiplied; they needed more tanks and more attention.

After two years the friend had enough of "cleaning and feeding and all of that stuff," and he decided to return the fish to their owner. To do that, he put them into little plastic bags, and drove them to Wisconsin. What made the trip even riskier was that he delivered them during winter. He drove half way, stayed overnight at a motel, and because he was afraid that the fish would freeze in the car he brought them into his room. Every fish made the trip from Massachusetts to Wisconsin successfully!

A CatFish Tale is loosely based on this amazing story — with minor alterations. The physician's role is played by Charlie the penguin and the friend is represented by the cat who is also the narrator.

I hope you have as much fun reading **A CatFish Tale** as I had writing it. As in all of my picture books, discussion questions follow the story.

Enjoy!

Kathy Brodsky

Kathy Brodsky
www.helpingwords.com

IT'S TRUE that the concept of each book is mine, and the writing is mine, but there are many people who help along the way. My picture books would be only words without the fantastic talent of artist Cameron Bennett. Cameron has given life, color and whimsy to every piece of every story. He is amazing! Others who have added bits and pieces to *A CatFish Tale* are: Richard (it's his story), Julia, Louise, Mary, Pamme, Colleen, Greg, Jeff, Barbara, Bedford Writers' Group, Karen at Printers Square, and Kim and Nick at wedü.

Thanks also to the wonderful folks who listened to the story, loved the pictures and laughed in all the right places.

Thank you one and all!

Publisher's Cataloging-in-Publication
(Provided by The Donohue Group, Inc.)

Brodsky, Kathy.
   A CatFish tale: loosely based on a true story / by Kathy Brodsky; illustrations by Cameron Bennett.
   p. : col. ill. ; cm.
   SUMMARY: A funny story in rhyme about a cat who was asked by his penguin friend to take care of the penguin's pet fish while the penguin went half way across the country to obtain a college degree. The cat took care of the fish for several years, then he drove the fish to the university so they could be reunited with their "dad." Discussion questions and activities follow the story
   Interest age group: 002–009.
   ISBN: 978-0-9828529-3-4

   1. Cats--Juvenile fiction. 2. Penguins--Juvenile fiction.
3. Friendship--Juvenile fiction. 4. Responsibility--Juvenile fiction.
5. Cats--Fiction. 6. Penguins--Fiction. 7. Friendship--Fiction.
8. Responsibility--Fiction. 9. Stories in rhyme. I. Bennett, Cameron (Cameron D.) II. Title

PZ8.3.B782   Cat 2012
[E]

A Horse Named Special, written by Kathy Brodsky and illustrated by Cameron Bennett, is the 2012 Picture Book of the Year! (Awarded by Creative Child Magazine)

Published by Helpingwords
A CatFish Tale © 2013
Printed in the U.S.A
Printed on recycled paper

Kathy Brodsky
www.kathybrodsky.com
Manchester, NH 03104
ISBN: 978-0-9828529-3-4